OLIVER PIG
AND THE
BEST FORT EVER

by Jean Van Leeuwen
pictures by Ann Schweninger

DIAL BOOKS FOR YOUNG READERS

For David, once more
—J. V. L.

For Ron
—A. S.

DIAL BOOKS FOR YOUNG READERS • A division of Penguin Young Readers Group
Published by The Penguin Group • Penguin Group (USA) Inc., 375 Hudson Street, New York,
NY 10014, U.S.A. • Penguin Group (Canada), 90 Eglinton Avenue East, Suite 700, Toronto,
Ontario, Canada M4P 2Y3 (a division of Pearson Penguin Canada Inc.) • Penguin Books Ltd,
80 Strand, London WC2R 0RL, England • Penguin Ireland, 25 St. Stephen's Green, Dublin 2,
Ireland (a division of Penguin Books Ltd) • Penguin Group (Australia), 250 Camberwell Road,
Camberwell, Victoria 3124, Australia (a division of Pearson Australia Group Pty Ltd) • Penguin
Books India Pvt Ltd, 11 Community Centre, Panchsheel Park, New Delhi - 110 017, India
Penguin Group (NZ), Cnr Airborne and Rosedale Roads, Albany, Auckland 1310, New Zealand
(a division of Pearson New Zealand Ltd) • Penguin Books (South Africa) (Pty) Ltd, 24 Sturdee
Avenue, Rosebank, Johannesburg 2196, South Africa Penguin Books Ltd, Registered Offices:
80 Strand, London WC2R 0RL, England

10 9 8 7 6 5 4 3 2 1

Library of Congress Cataloging-in-Publication Data • Van Leeuwen, Jean. • Oliver Pig and the
best fort ever / by Jean Van Leeuwen ; pictures by Ann Schweninger. • p. cm. • Summary:
Oliver Pig decides to build a fort in the backyard and his friends become involved with the proj-
ect. ISBN 0-8037-2888-3 • [1. Building—Fiction. 2. Pigs—Fiction.] • I. Schweninger, Ann, ill.
II. Title. • PZ7.V3273Omj 2006 • [E]—dc22 • 2004014963

*The full-color artwork was prepared using carbon pencil,
colored pencils, and watercolor washes.*

Reading Level 1.9

CONTENTS

THE FORT

"Today," said Oliver,

"I am going to build a fort.

It will be my biggest, tallest,

strongest, best fort ever."

"Can I help?" asked Amanda.

"No," said Oliver. "This is my fort."

Oliver found a good spot for his fort

by the back fence.

"Now, what can I use to build it?"

he wondered.

Oliver looked around.

"Rocks would be good," he said.

He carried six big rocks to his fort.

Oliver looked behind the garage.

"Bricks would be great," he said.

He loaded them into his wagon.

"Now I can build a wall."

He piled the bricks on top of the rocks.

But the wall wasn't very high.

And it kept falling down.

"I need some wood," he said.

Oliver saw the back fence.

"If only that fence was falling down,"

he said, "I could use the boards."

But the fence wasn't falling down.

Oliver saw Father's garden.

"If only I could use those tall poles,"

he said.

But Father would be angry.

And the tomato plants would fall over.

Oliver saw the picnic table.

"Oh, boy!" he said.

"If only I could use that table.

I could make the biggest, tallest,

strongest, best fort ever."

But Mother would be angry.

And they could never have a picnic.

Oliver walked to the front yard.

He saw a pine branch

that the wind had knocked down.

He saw sticks under the apple tree.

"Finally," he said, "I found some wood."

Oliver dragged the wood to his fort.

He piled the branch and sticks

on top of the rocks and bricks.

Then he sat inside his new fort.

It was a tight squeeze.

The sticks were poking him.

The pine needles were tickling him.

And if he moved, his fort might fall down.

Amanda came outside.

"Is that your best fort ever?" she said.

She laughed.

"You didn't make a fort," she said.

"You made a nest."

THE BEST FORT EVER

Albert and James came over

to play in Oliver's fort.

"My feet are sticking out," said James.

"Move over, Oliver."

Oliver moved over.

"Now my whole body is sticking out,"

said Albert. "Move over, Oliver."

Oliver moved over again.

"Now you're sitting on me," said James.

"And I'm all curled up like a snail,"

said Albert.

He stretched.

"Uh-oh," said Oliver.

"Watch out!" said James.

The fort fell down.

"It's too bad about your fort," said Albert.

"It was too small," said James.

"I know," said Oliver.

"But I don't have enough stuff to make it bigger."

"Hmmm," said Albert.

"I think I have an idea."

"Hmmm," said James. "Me too.

See you later, Oliver."

Albert and James went home.

"Father," said Oliver,

"I need more stuff to build my fort.

Do you have any old junk I could use?"

"Let's look in the garage," said Father.

The garage was full of old junk.

"You can have those boards,"

said Father. "And that broom

and that hose and those tires."

"This is good junk," said Oliver.

"Thanks, Father!"

"Thank you!" said Father.

"You helped me clean out the garage."

Oliver carried the boards and broom

and hose and tires to his fort.

"Hey, Oliver," said Albert.

"Look what I found."

He was carrying the biggest box

Oliver had ever seen.

"Super!" said Oliver.

"I found a box too," said James.

"And a blanket. And some poles.

We could make a teepee."

"Great!" said Oliver.

"And look at all the good junk I found."

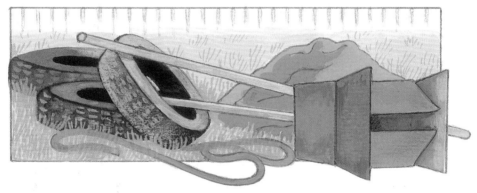

Oliver and Albert and James

started to build.

"Your new fort will be so big,"

said James, "that we can all fit inside.

We won't have to curl up like snails."

"It will be so tall," said Albert,

"that I can even stand up."

"And it will be so strong," said Oliver,

"that it will never fall down."

"It will have a teepee," said James.

"And a tunnel," said Albert.

"And maybe even a tower," said Oliver.

"This is going to be my best fort ever!"

NO GIRLS ALLOWED

Oliver and Albert and James

were working on Oliver's fort.

"The big box will be the fort,"

said Oliver. "And the little box

can be a look-out tower on top."

"Good idea," said Albert.

"Can I help?" asked Amanda.

"No," said Oliver.

"No girls allowed," said Albert.

"Go away," said James.

Amanda went away. But not very far.

"She's still there," said James.

"Pretend you don't see her," said Oliver.

"We need some rope," said Albert.

"You can use my jump rope,"

said Amanda.

"We told you to go away," said Oliver.

"We told you no girls allowed,"

said Albert.

"And no little kids either," said James.

"I'm not a little kid," said Amanda.

She went away. But not very far.

"I bet she is still there," said Albert.

"I bet she is spying on us."

"Are you spying, Amanda?" called Oliver.

"You know what we do to spies,"

said Albert.

"Specially little kid girl spies," said James.

Amanda went inside.

"She's really gone this time," said Albert.

"Good," said Oliver. "Now we can build."

They made the tires into a tunnel.

They made the blanket and poles

into a teepee.

They made windows in the look-out tower.

The fort was almost finished.

"All we need is a flag," said Albert.

"We can make it out of that broom."

"I'm so hot!" said Oliver.

"Building a fort is hard work."

"We need a drink," said Albert.

Amanda and her friend Lollipop

were drinking lemonade

under the apple tree.

"Quick," said James,

"give us some lemonade!"

"You can't have our lemonade,"

said Amanda.

"Please?" said Oliver.

"No," said Lollipop.

"No boys allowed under the apple tree,"
said Amanda. "And no big kids."

"You're mean," said Oliver.

"I know," said Amanda.

"But you were mean first."

"Really really mean," said Lollipop.

"Maybe," said Amanda,

"we might give you some

if you let us see your fort."

"I'm so thirsty," said James,

"I could drink a whole ocean."

"Okay," said Oliver.

"You can come see our fort.

But you can't help build it."

"Who wants to help build it?"

said Lollipop. "It's too hot."

So they crawled through the tunnel.

And Oliver and Albert and James

and Amanda and Lollipop

all had lemonade in Oliver's fort.

THE CAMP OUT

The flag was up.

Oliver's fort was finally finished.

"Wow!" said Oliver.

"This really is my best fort ever."

Oliver and Albert and James

played in it all day.

"I wish we could live in your fort

all the time," said Albert.

"My mother and father wouldn't let me,"

said James.

"Me either," said Oliver.

"But we could camp out in it all night."

"Yes!" said Albert and James.

So that night they had a camp-out.

"What is all that stuff?" asked Oliver.

"It's just my sleeping bag," said Albert.

"And my pajamas and toothbrush

and a few bug books

and my bug collection."

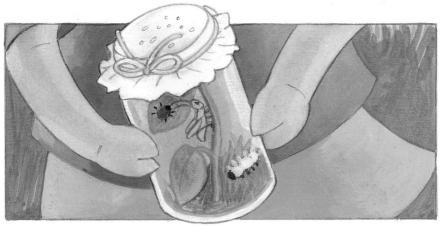

"You brought your bugs?" said James.

"They would be lonely without me,"

said Albert.

Father gave them a flashlight.

Mother gave them a bag of cookies.

"Have a good time," she said.

Oliver and Albert and James

crawled into Oliver's fort.

"Let's not go to sleep," said Albert.

"We can stay awake all night,"

said James.

"Okay," said Oliver.

They ate cookies and talked.

Oliver told jokes.

Albert told silly bug riddles.

James told a scary ghost story.

Just then Oliver felt something move next to his foot.

Was it a ghost?

He jumped up.

He turned on his flashlight.

"It's a snake!" he cried. "A big one!"

Albert and James jumped up too.

The snake was big, all right.

But it wasn't moving.

"Oh," said Oliver.

"It's just Father's old hose."

They got back in their sleeping bags.

"What shall we do now?" asked James.

Oliver couldn't think of anything.

His eyes kept closing.

Just then something pinched him.

"Stop that!" he said.

"Stop what?" said James.

"Pinching me," said Oliver.

"And tickling me," said Albert.

"I'm not pinching or tickling,"

said James.

Oliver and Albert and James jumped up.

"My bugs!" cried Albert. "They escaped!"

The bugs were everywhere.

They tried to catch them.

"I got one!" said James.

He tripped over Albert.

Albert knocked over Oliver.

Suddenly there was a big crash.

"Uh-oh," said Oliver.

They crawled out of the fort.

"Our tower fell down," said Albert.

"And the teepee fell over," said James.

"My fort is wrecked," said Oliver.

He knocked on the back door.

"What's wrong?" said Father.

"Can we sleep inside?" asked Oliver.

"Of course," said Father.

So Oliver and Albert and James

had a camp-in on the porch.

"Tomorrow we'll rebuild your fort,"

said Albert.

"Maybe," said Oliver,

"we could even make it into a castle."